Green Light Readers
For the new reader who's ready to GO!

Amazing adventures await every young child who is eager to read.
Green Light Readers encourage children to explore, to imagine, and to grow through books. Created for beginning readers at two levels of skill, these lively illustrated stories have been carefully developed to reinforce reading basics taught at school and to make reading a fun and rewarding experience for children and grown-ups to share outside the classroom.

The grades and ages within each skill level are general guidelines only, and books included in both levels may feature any or all of the bulleted characteristics. When choosing a book for a new reader, remember that every child progresses at his or her own pace—be patient and supportive as the magic of reading takes hold.

❶ Buckle up!
Kindergarten–Grade 1: Developing reading skills, ages 5–7
- Short, simple stories • Fully illustrated • Familiar objects and situations
- Playful rhythms • Spoken language patterns of children
- Rhymes and repeated phrases • Strong link between text and art

2 Start the engine!
Grades 1–2: Reading with help, ages 6–8
- Longer stories, including nonfiction • Short chapters
- Generously illustrated • Less-familiar situations
- More fully developed characters • Creative language, including dialogue
- More subtle link between text and art

Green Light Readers incorporate characteristics detailed in the Reading Recovery model used by educators to assess the readability of texts through the end of first grade. Guidelines for reading levels for these readers have been developed with assistance from Mary Lou Meerson. An educational consultant, Ms. Meerson has been a classroom teacher, a language arts coordinator, an elementary school principal, and a university professor.

Published in collaboration with Harcourt School Publishers

Jack and Rick

Jack and Rick

David McPhail

Green Light Readers
Harcourt, Inc.
San Diego   New York   London

www.harcourt.com

First Green Light Readers edition 2002
Green Light Readers is a trademark of Harcourt, Inc., registered in the United States of America and/or other jurisdictions.

Library of Congress Cataloging-in-Publication Data
McPhail, David M.
Jack and Rick/David McPhail.
p. cm.
"Green Light Readers."
Summary: Jack and Rick want to play together, but there's a river between them and they will have to work together to bridge it.
[1. Cooperativeness—Fiction. 2. Friendship—Fiction.] I. Title. II. Series.
PZ7.M2427Jac 2002
[E]—dc21 2001002369
ISBN 0-15-216552-5
ISBN 0-15-216540-1 (pb)

A C E G H F D B
A C E G H F D B (pb)

Jack and Rick want to play.

Can Jack pick up the log?

No, it's too big!

Can Rick help Jack?

Yes, Rick can pass the rope.

Can they lift it now?

Yes, they can.

Can Rick walk to Jack?

No! Oh no!

Can Jack help Rick?

Yes, Jack can help.

Now, Jack and Rick can play.

Meet the Author-Illustrator

David McPhail loves the way Jack and Rick work together as a team. He says, "I like the way the characters in this story find a way to get on the same side of the stream—even though it's not easy." He hopes you help your friends the way Jack and Rick helped each other!

David McPhail